Mr Moo...
I Want You

Illustrated by Julia Seal

Picture Corgi

Bella was a very lucky little girl. She had a lovely mummy and daddy, and a big brother, Daniel, who always looked after her. And she had the very best friend in the world . . . Mr Moo.

Mr Moo...
I Want You

Read more books in this series:

Mr Moo . . . Aaaachoooo!

Mr Moo . . . What Shall We Do?

Mr Moo . . . I Love You Too

MR MOO . . . I WANT YOU
A PICTURE CORGI BOOK 978 0 552 57614 7
Published in Great Britain
by Picture Corgi, an imprint of Random House Children's Publishers UK
A Random House Group Company
This edition published 2014

3 5 7 9 10 8 6 4 2

Picture Corgi Books are published by Random House Children's Publishers UK,
61–63 Uxbridge Road, London W5 5SA
www.randomhousechildrens.co.uk
www.randomhouse.co.uk
Addresses for companies within The Random House Group Limited can be found at:
www.randomhouse.co.uk/offices.htm
THE RANDOM HOUSE GROUP Limited Reg. No. 954009
A CIP catalogue record for this book is available from the British Library.
Printed in China

Bella and Mr Moo did everything together. Mr Moo always knew just what Bella was thinking, and he was always there to have fun with, to share stories with and to give advice.

Mr Moo loved it best when Bella told the story of how they had met for the very first time.

"One day, before I knew you, Mr Moo, the whole family went out together," said Bella. "We walked past the toy shop and I saw someone waving from the window . . .

The Bakery

Open

Tom's Toy Shop

It was *you*, Mr Moo, but Mum said we would be late.
So we carried on over the road to the park.

We spent all day in the sun. I played on the swings with Daniel and my friends, Nadia and Ellie. But the whole time I couldn't stop thinking about the colourful cow I had seen.

On the way home, we walked past the toy shop again, but I couldn't see you, Mr Moo.

I knew that I *just had* to go inside to see if you were there. Mum said we could go in, but just to look.

There were lots of new toys that I had never seen before, and I couldn't see you anywhere.

Then, suddenly, as if by magic, there was the one toy that I knew I wanted. A funny, colourful cow – it was you, Mr Moo!

I wanted you more than anything, but I had promised
just to look and not ask for anything.
Daniel used his pocket money to buy a big cuddly
dinosaur, but I didn't have any pocket money.
It was so hard to leave you behind.

All the way back down the high street I felt as if there was someone following me. And I even thought I heard my name. But when I looked, there was nobody there.

When we got home, Daniel asked if I wanted to
play with his new dinosaur, but I didn't feel like it.
I couldn't stop thinking about you, Mr Moo,
and I sat here in my room feeling sad.

Suddenly I heard a knock on the door. It was Dad –
he had something colourful under his arm.
It was you, Mr Moo. It was *you*!
"Someone saw what a good girl you were today
and followed us home," said Dad.

From then on we had fun every day, didn't we, Mr Moo," said Bella, giving Mr Moo a squeeze. And Bella and Mr Moo thought about all the great things they had done together.

Bella was a very lucky girl indeed,
and Mr Moo was very lucky too!